Something's Fishy

For Orit, Kathie, and Cindy—the most
supportive mermaids I know—N. K.

For Michael—a big fish in our
little pond!—J&W

GROSSET & DUNLAP
Published by the Penguin Group
Penguin Group (USA) Inc., 375 Hudson Street,
New York, New York 10014, U.S.A.
Penguin Group (Canada), 90 Eglinton Avenue East, Suite 700, Toronto,
Ontario, Canada M4P 2Y3 (a division of Pearson Penguin Canada Inc.)
Penguin Books Ltd, 80 Strand, London WC2R 0RL, England
Penguin Ireland, 25 St Stephen's Green, Dublin 2,
Ireland (a division of Penguin Books Ltd)
Penguin Group (Australia), 250 Camberwell Road, Camberwell,
Victoria 3124, Australia (a division of Pearson Australia Group Pty Ltd)
Penguin Books India Pvt Ltd, 11 Community Centre,
Panchsheel Park, New Delhi - 110 017, India
Penguin Group (NZ), 67 Apollo Drive, Rosedale, North Shore 0745, Auckland,
New Zealand (a division of Pearson New Zealand Ltd)
Penguin Books (South Africa) (Pty) Ltd, 24 Sturdee Avenue, Rosebank,
Johannesburg 2196, South Africa

Penguin Books Ltd, Registered Offices:
80 Strand, London WC2R 0RL, England

Text copyright © 2007 by Nancy Krulik. Illustrations copyright © 2007 by John
and Wendy. All rights reserved. Published by Grosset & Dunlap, a division of
Penguin Young Readers Group, 345 Hudson Street, New York, New York 10014.
GROSSET & DUNLAP is a trademark of Penguin Group (USA) Inc.
Printed in the U.S.A.

Library of Congress Control Number: 2007007024

ISBN 978-0-448-44442-0   10 9 8 7 6 5 4 3

Something's Fishy

by Nancy Krulik • illustrated by John & Wendy

Grosset & Dunlap

Chapter 1

"Welcome to school," Mr. Guthrie greeted Katie Carew as she walked into her classroom on Monday morning. "All fish travel in schools. This is right where you belong."

"But I'm not a fish . . ." Katie started to say. Then she stopped herself. As she looked around she saw that her classroom had turned into some sort of underwater world.

Of course, Katie wasn't *really* underwater. Mr. G. had just decorated the classroom to make it look like a giant aquarium. Her teacher was always doing things like that.

"Let me guess, we're studying fish now," Andy Epstein said.

"You're a wise little guppy," Mr. G. told him.

Katie looked around the room. Mr. G. sure had worked hard. The walls were lined with giant photographs of fish and coral. The floor was covered with a sea green carpet. There were fish-shaped balloons hanging from the ceiling.

Mr. G. had even surrounded Slinky's cage with blue and green streamers. It looked as though Slinky were a sea snake, instead of a snake who was the class pet.

"Do we get to decorate our beanbags now?" Kevin Camilleri asked excitedly.

"You sure do, dude!" Mr. G. told him. "You'll find everything you need in the art corner."

Katie clapped her hands. Decorating her beanbag was always the most fun part of starting a new learning adventure. Mr. G. called all lessons learning adventures. And he called the kids dudes, instead of students.

Mr. G. didn't talk like other teachers.

He didn't act like other teachers, either. All of the kids in Mr. G.'s class sat in beanbag chairs. Mr. G. thought kids learned better when they were comfortable. Katie definitely agreed. And the beanbags were just one of the cool things Mr. G. did for his students. He also let the kids play games, cook, and tell jokes in the classroom. It was never boring in class 4A.

Sometimes Katie felt sorry for the kids in class 4B. Their teacher, Ms. Sweet, was really nice. But she was no Mr. G.

"Hey, do you guys know which fish is the most valuable?" George Brennan asked.

"No, which?" George's best pal, Kevin, asked.

"A *gold*fish," George answered. He laughed really hard at his own joke.

The other kids laughed, too. Well, all the kids except Kadeem Carter. He wasn't about to let George tell the only fish joke today.

"What do fish get when they graduate from

school?" Kadeem asked the other kids.

"What?" Emma Stavros asked him.

"A deep-ploma!" Kadeem shouted out. "Get it? *Deep* water?"

The other kids laughed. But not George. Katie could tell George was trying to think of a joke to top Kadeem's. All of a sudden he smiled in triumph.

"Yeah, I get it," George said. "And now I'm throwing it back."

"The laughs were too small to keep," Kevin added.

"Now here's a *real* joke," George told the class. "What kind of fish goes best with peanut butter?"

"What kind?" Mandy Banks wondered.

"*Jelly*fish!" George exclaimed.

"Sounds like we've got a great joke-off going on here!" Mr. G. chuckled. "Kadeem, it's your turn."

Kadeem stopped taping a Styrofoam fish eye to his beanbag long enough to say, "What part of a fish weighs the most?"

"What part?" Andy asked him.

"The scales!" Kadeem joked.

Everyone laughed at that—even George.

"Good one," Mr. G. chuckled. "Now finish up with your beanbags, everyone. I want to get started on this amazing learning adventure!"

$$\times \quad \times \quad \times$$

The kids in class 4A were all in very good moods when they got to lunch later that morning. Learning about fish could be a lot of fun!

"After lunch we are each going to get assigned a fish to study," Katie explained to her best friend Jeremy Fox. Jeremy was in class 4B.

"And then Mr. G. told us we're going to play this really great game where we get to pretend to *be* our fish," Kevin added.

"Big deal," Katie's other best friend, Suzanne Lock, said. She sat down across from Katie and Jeremy. "You should see the pretty aquarium Ms. Sweet brought in for our classroom."

"Our classroom *is* an aquarium," George said. "Mr. G. decorated every inch of it. You almost feel like you're underwater when you're in class 4A!"

Katie watched Suzanne's face fall. Her best friend really hated it when someone topped her. And she could be pretty mean when it happened.

"That's perfect for you, George. You smell like a fish. You should be in an aquarium," Suzanne told him.

Katie sighed. That was *such* a typical Suzanne thing to say.

"Of course in our class, we had a *really* awesome surprise," Suzanne continued. "One that's a lot cooler than fish stuff."

"What's so cool?" Mandy Banks asked, tugging at Suzanne's sleeve.

"Ms. Sweet is getting married!" Miriam Chan announced before Suzanne could get the words out.

Wow! Katie thought. That *was* big news.

"I was just going to tell them that!" Suzanne snapped at Miriam.

"Oops. Sorry," Miriam apologized.

"And, that's not all," Suzanne boasted to the kids in class 4A. "We're having an engagement party for Ms. Sweet."

"We are?" Jessica Haynes asked Suzanne. "Who says?"

"I do," Suzanne told her. "I just decided it. Of course it's only for *our* class."

Katie frowned. She hated it when Suzanne left her out of things.

"You understand, don't you, Katie?" Suzanne asked her.

Katie shrugged, but she didn't answer.

"I mean Ms. Sweet is *our* teacher, not yours," Suzanne reminded her. She smiled triumphantly. "It's going to be a really great party. I bet that makes all you kids in 4A wish you were in our class."

"We do not wish that!" Katie exclaimed suddenly. "We don't wish anything!"

Everyone looked at Katie. *They probably think I'm crazy,* she thought to herself. *But I'm not. I just know that wishes can be terrible things.*

Chapter 2

Last year, in third grade, Katie had learned all about wishes. It started one terrible, horrible day, when Katie had missed the football and lost the game for her team. Then she'd fallen in a big mud puddle and ruined her favorite pair of jeans. Even worse, she'd let out a huge burp in front of the whole class. How embarrassing!

That night, Katie had wished she could be anyone but herself. There must have been a shooting star overhead or something, because the next day the magic wind came.

The magic wind was a super-strong, tornado-like wind that blew only around Katie.

It was so powerful that
every time it came, it
turned Katie into some-
one else.

The first time the
magic wind came it
turned Katie into
Speedy, the class 3A
hamster. She'd escaped
from her cage, and
wound up inside George's stinky sneaker. *Yuck!*

Since then, the magic wind had been back
again and again. One time it turned her into
Mr. Starkey, the school music teacher. The
band sounded really terrible when Katie was
the conductor!

Katie still got embarrassed thinking about
the time the magic wind switcherooed her into
her favorite author, Nellie Farrow. Nellie had
come to talk to the fourth grade about her
new book. The trouble was, Katie hadn't read
the book yet. Because of Katie, Nellie had

looked like a fool in front of everybody!

And once, Katie had turned into Jeremy's kitten, Lucky. That time her own cocker spaniel, Pepper, chased her right up a tree. Katie didn't blame Pepper, though. After all, cats and dogs just don't get along.

Not that it was any better the time Katie turned into Pepper himself. She'd gotten into a nasty argument with a squirrel and destroyed her next-door neighbor's lawn. And poor Pepper was the one blamed.

That was the worst thing about the magic wind. Every time it came, whoever Katie turned into got in big trouble. Then it was up to Katie to make things all right again. And that wasn't always so easy.

So now Katie didn't make wishes anymore. She stayed far, far away from them. They caused too many problems.

But of course she couldn't explain that to her friends. So instead, she just told the other kids, "I meant we like our class a lot, too."

"Yeah," George agreed. "We have fun every day. Not just on special occasions."

"Exactly," Emma Weber agreed. "Class 4A is really great."

"Maybe." Suzanne shrugged. "But our party is going to be incredible. Nothing is going to top it."

Chapter 3

"Andy, you're a grouper. That's a predator fish," Mr. G. said as he walked around the room after lunch. He was assigning everyone their fish to research. "Emma Stavros, you're an angelfish."

"That's because I'm always so good," Emma S. said with a smile.

"Kadeem, you're a red snapper," Mr. G. continued. "Mandy, you're an anthias."

"Anthias? I never heard of that fish," Mandy said.

"And Kevin, you're a frog fish," said Mr. G.

"A frog?" Kevin asked curiously. "Like the ones that say *rrbit, rrbit*? They're not fish!"

"You're a frog *fish*," Mr. G. corrected him. "I think you'll find them interesting. They're tough predators. They swallow their prey faster than almost any other fish."

"That sounds like you, Kev," George joked. "You eat faster than anyone. Even me. You ate that whole pint of grape tomatoes in five minutes last week."

"Yeah, but tomatoes aren't fish food," Kevin reminded him. "At least I don't think they are."

"You'll find out what's on a frog fish menu when you do your research," Mr. G. told him. He turned to Emma W. "You're a predator, too," he told her. "A swordfish."

Katie couldn't help but laugh. It was funny to think of sweet Emma Weber as a vicious swordfish.

"George, you're a herring," Mr. G. told him. "And Katie, you're a clown fish."

"Hey, Mr. G., don't you think I should be the clown fish?" George argued with his teacher. "I *am* the funniest guy in the whole school!"

"Hey!" Kadeem argued.

"Well, I am," George insisted. "Can't Katie be a herring instead?"

Mr. G. shook his head. "Nope. No trading. But I think you'll like being a herring." The teacher pulled a silver and green kazoo from his pocket. "You get to use this."

"A kazoo? Why?" George asked.

"Well, herrings make a funny noise when they're communicating with each other," Mr. G. said. "It kind of sounds like they're passing gas."

"Oh man!" Kadeem laughed. "George's fish likes to cut the cheese!"

Everyone laughed.

George frowned. "Now I *really* think Katie should be a herring. She's Katie Kazoo, remember?"

Katie smiled. How could anybody forget? George had given her that way-cool nickname last year, and it had stuck ever since.

But Katie didn't want to be a fish with gas. No way!

"Okay, we'll spend most of this afternoon researching our fish in the library," Mr. G. said. "And then tomorrow, we'll play Capture the Prey!"

"How do you play that?" Mandy asked.

"Well, it's sort of like tag," Mr. G. told her. "The three predator fish have to catch all of the prey fish. It's up to the prey fish to stay away and keep safe."

"Oh, that sounds like fun!" Emma W. exclaimed. "I love playing tag."

"Me too!" Katie told her. "But I'm not going to let you catch me just because we're friends."

"Don't worry," Emma W. said. "I'll eat the other kids first." She grinned. "You can be my dessert."

"Clown fish are really cool," Katie told Jeremy as the fourth-grade kids walked out of school together at the end of the day. "They're reddish-orange. My hair is almost the same color as they are—except the fish have three white stripes on them. I won't get that in my hair until I'm really old."

Jeremy laughed. Katie giggled, too. It was funny picturing herself as an old lady with streaks of white in her red hair.

Just then, George walked by, tooting his kazoo.

"What's that for?" Becky Stern asked him.

"You wouldn't understand," George told her. "It's a herring thing."

"George is right," Kevin agreed. "Herrings

have a funny way of talking to one another."

The kids in class 4A all started to laugh. The kids in class 4B just looked at one another.

Suddenly Suzanne bent down and pulled some ugly green weeds from the grass. Then she began walking slowly down the path that led to the sidewalk. As she walked, she threw pieces of weeds to her left and to her right.

"What are you doing?" Katie asked her.

"I'm practicing being a flower girl," Suzanne told her.

"Ms. Sweet asked you to be the flower girl in her wedding?" Miriam asked Suzanne.

"Not exactly," Suzanne admitted. "But she might. And I want to be prepared."

Katie sighed. Somehow she doubted that was going to happen. But she didn't tell Suzanne that. No sense making her angry.

"I think this whole wedding thing is soooooo romantic," Becky cooed. She looked over at Jeremy. "Do you ever think about your wedding, Jeremy?"

Jeremy's cheeks turned bright red. "No," he mumbled. "I'm only ten years old."

"I think about it all the time," Becky told him. "I want a white dress with lots of lace. And a really long veil. Don't you think I'll look pretty in lace, Jeremy?"

Jeremy blushed harder and turned away.

"Oh, Jeremy," George said, imitating Becky. "Won't I be a gorgeous bride?"

"Cut it out, George," Jeremy grumbled.

"Mrs. Becky Fox," Kevin added. "It has a nice ring to it."

"*I* think so," Becky said.

"Or maybe you could be Mrs. Rebecca Fox. That's so much more grown-up," Miriam suggested.

George and Kevin giggled.

Jeremy groaned.

Katie felt really bad for Jeremy. Everyone knew Becky had a huge crush on Jeremy. But Jeremy didn't like Becky at all. And he hated it when she flirted with him, like she was

doing now.

"Um, Jeremy, don't you have soccer practice today?" Katie asked him. "I think you'd better get home."

"Yeah, I guess so," Jeremy said. He smiled gratefully at Katie.

"I'll come with you," Katie told him. Then she and Jeremy ran off, getting as far as they could—as *fast* as they could—from all that wedding talk.

Chapter 4

"Okay, now when I blow this whistle, Andy, Kevin, and Emma W. will try to tag as many of you as possible," Mr. G. told the kids in class 4A on Tuesday morning. They were all lined up, ready to play Capture the Prey. "If you are tagged, you have to go stand at the edge of the sea . . . I mean the field," he explained.

As soon as Mr. G. blew his whistle, Katie and the other 4A fish scattered across the field. They moved as fast as their fins . . . *er* . . . legs could carry them. But some of the fish just weren't fast enough.

"Gotcha!" Andy shouted as he tagged

Emma S. on the back.

"Gotcha!" Emma W. called out as she caught up with Kadeem and tagged him on the arm.

"Watch out, George, I'm coming for you!" Kevin warned his best friend.

Toot! Toot! George began playing his kazoo loudly as he ran.

"Hey, what's that smell?" Kadeem asked. He pinched his nostrils tight. "It stinks like rotten fish. Must be George's tooter."

Katie giggled. It sure did sound like George was passing gas.

"What are you doing, George?" Kevin asked him.

"I'm calling to the other fish for help," George replied. *Toot. Toot.*

"Sorry, George, that won't work," Mr. G. called onto the field. "Only herrings can hear that sound. And you're the only herring in the sea today."

"Not anymore," Kevin said, tagging George

on the shoulder. "This sea is now herring free. You've been eaten by the mighty frog fish, buddy."

"Spit him out," Kadeem shouted. "I'll bet he tastes as nasty as he sounds!"

George turned and blew his kazoo at Kadeem. "What are you laughing at?" George asked him. "You were tagged by a *girl* fish!"

"I'm not just a girl, I'm a *swordfish* girl," Emma W. said proudly. She chomped her teeth up and down ferociously. "Every fish in the sea is afraid of me!"

"Watch out, Mandy. You're about to be eaten!" Kevin cried out.

Katie shook her head. That was a bad move on Kevin's part. Mandy was the fastest girl in the whole grade. He never should have given her any warning. She'd started running as soon as Kevin went after her. Now there was no way Kevin could catch her.

But Emma W. could. It wasn't that Emma W. was a fast runner. It was just that Mandy was so focused on keeping away from Kevin, she didn't see Andy and Emma W. at the other end of the field.

Emma W. was right there, ready to tag Mandy as she ran by.

"Gotcha!" Emma W. told Mandy.

"Oh yeah! Teamwork!" Kevin shouted out, giving Emma W. a big high five.

"And now we three can go after Katie!" Emma W. told Kevin and Andy. "Three against one. We're sure to get her!"

"Look out, Katie Kazoo, we're coming for you!" Kevin warned.

But Katie didn't move. She stood right where she was with a big smile on her face.

"You'd better get running!" Emma W. told her.

Katie reached into her jacket pocket and pulled out a white sponge with pipe-cleaner tentacles coming out of it.

"You guys had better not come near me," Katie warned the predators. "This is my sea anemone."

"No, Katie. *I'm* your sea enemy," Andy told her. "And I'm gonna swallow you up whole!"

"That's sea *anemone*," Katie corrected Andy. "It's a sea animal that has lots of tentacles. The tentacles sting any fish that come near it . . . except for clown fish. This sea anemone is like my base. As long as I'm near it, you can't tag me."

"Hey, that's not fair!" Kevin insisted. "There's no base in the sea. You're not safe anywhere."

Katie looked over at Mr. G. He smiled at her and punched his fist in the air.

"Who says?" Katie asked. "In the real ocean, clown fish can hide in sea anemones.

That's how they survive."

"Mr. G., Katie's cheating," Kevin whined.

"I am not," Katie told him.

"But there's no way we can capture you as long as you're with that sea anemone," Emma W. insisted.

"Exactly," Katie told her proudly. "You'll just have to swim somewhere else for your dinner."

"Hey, quit clowning around," Kevin insisted.

"I'm a *clown* fish. That's what I'm supposed to do," Katie said with a laugh.

"Sorry, frog fish," Mr. G. told Kevin. "Seems Katie the clown fish has figured out a way to beat the predators."

"That makes me the winner!" Katie cheered. She was really happy. Katie wasn't a very fast runner. She hardly ever won at games like this.

"Actually, you're *all* winners," Mr. G. told the class.

"Huh?" George wondered.

"I've got a big prize for all of you," Mr. G. said. "It's something fish like you will really love."

"What, worms for lunch?" Kadeem wondered.

Mr. G laughed. "No. You can still eat the macaroni and cheese in the cafeteria," he assured Kadeem. "Actually, your prize is a trip to the Cherrydale Aquarium. You can see real fish swimming in their natural environments. We'll be going tomorrow with class 4B."

"Oh yeah! The aquarium!" Kevin cheered. "I can't wait to see a real live frog fish."

Toot. Toot. George blew on his kazoo.

"What was that for?" Mandy asked him.

"I'm just sending a message to the herrings at the Cherrydale Aquarium," George replied. "Get ready, guys. The big tooter is on his way!"

Chapter 5

"I want to find some clown fish!" Katie shouted out excitedly as she peered into the glass that enclosed the giant tank at the Cherrydale Aquarium. It was shaped like a giant glass cylinder, even taller than Katie's house. You could walk up a ramp and see stuff from all different angles.

"The Great Barrier Reef tank is really beautiful," Emma W. added. "There's a star-fish and a crab and . . ."

"Did you know clown fish can live up to five years?" Katie asked Suzanne and Miriam, who were walking with her. "That's a really long time for fish. And they got their name because their coloring is sort of clownlike, and . . ."

"Whatever," Suzanne said, rolling her eyes.

"Don't you think this is fun?" Katie asked her best friend.

"Sure," Suzanne assured her. "It's just that I have so much more on my mind. I'm thinking about the food we'll have and the games we'll play at the class 4B engagement party."

Katie sighed. Once again, Suzanne was

making her feel left out. And she wasn't the only one. From the look on Emma W.'s face, Katie could tell she was kind of sad about it, too. Then suddenly Katie saw a small flash of orange, black, and white swim past.

"Hello, clown fish! I'm a clown fish, too!" Katie said, pushing her face up against the aquarium glass. But the clown fish didn't even seem to notice Katie.

"I think you're taking this be-a-fish thing too seriously," Suzanne said. "You're not *really* a clown fish, Katie."

"Hey, it's me! Katie Kazoo, Clown Fish Girl!" Katie said louder. But the fish didn't look her way.

"I don't think it can hear you through the glass," Jeremy told her.

"Come on, over here," Katie urged the fish, tapping on the glass to get its attention.

That worked. The little fish looked startled and then swam away . . . *right in the direction of a gray shark!*

"Oh no!" Katie cried out. "A shark! Watch out, clown fish!"

At the very last minute, the orange-and-white fish changed direction and swam off, hiding itself in a sea anemone's tentacles. The nurse shark swam off without even bothering it.

"Wow! That was close!" George said.

"You're not kidding," Kevin said. "A few more seconds and that clown fish would have been a shark's supper."

Katie frowned. And it would have been all her fault.

"Luckily that sea anemone was there," Emma W. told Katie.

"Come on, dudes," Mr. G. urged the kids. "Let's go up to the top of the aquarium so you can look down into the top of the tank."

Katie and her friends followed Mr. G. up the winding ramp around the tank until they reached the top. They stopped right in front of a protective railing.

"Okay, guys, now take a look," Mr. G. said.

Katie did. "Oh wow!" she exclaimed as she looked into the water. The fish had looked beautiful before when she'd been looking at them through the glass. But now, staring down at the whole Great Barrier Reef, with nothing between herself and the fish, well . . .

"This is the most beautiful thing I've ever seen," Emma W. told Katie.

Katie nodded. That was exactly what she'd been thinking.

"Check out that diver down there," Kevin said. "He just fed a shark!"

"Man, he's really brave!" Andy exclaimed.

"What's that funny ball over there?" George asked, pointing. "The white one with the pointy things coming out of it."

"That's a porcupine fish," Ms. Sweet told him. "He must feel threatened by the shark. When porcupine fish are scared, they swallow a lot of water so they blow up like a balloon. Their quills stick out all over. It makes them really hard to eat."

"Cool," George said. "Hey, look at me. I'm a porcupine fish." Then he took a big sip of water from his bottle and held it in his cheeks. But when he coughed, the water spurted out of his mouth and all over his shirt.

"Gross, George," Suzanne said with a sigh.

"Oh, look at those blue-and-black fish," Emma S. said. "They're gorgeous."

"I wish we could see them closer," Katie said. "We're so high, and they're swimming so close to the bottom of the tank."

"I can make them come closer," Kevin said. "When I feed my goldfish, they always swim up to the top of the tank to get the food." He reached into his lunch bag and pulled a piece of bread from his sandwich.

"That's a good idea, Kevin," Katie said. "They're probably hungry, anyway."

"Exactly," Kevin agreed. "Here, little fishies. Come and get it!"

"Kevin, don't!" Ms. Sweet warned and

came running over. She lunged for his hand before he could drop any bread into the tank.

"But I was just . . ." Kevin began.

Before he could finish his sentence, Ms. Sweet let out a loud gasp. She was staring at her hand. "Oh no!" she cried out. "My engagement ring. It's gone!"

Chapter 6

Mr. G. came racing over. "Are you sure you were wearing the ring? Maybe you left it home this morning?" he asked Ms. Sweet hopefully.

Ms. Sweet shook her head. "That ring hasn't left my finger since I got it . . . at least not until now," she added sorrowfully.

Katie had never seen a teacher so upset. Ms. Sweet almost looked as if she was going to cry.

"It must have fallen off when I pulled Kevin away from the tank," Ms. Sweet said, staring at her hand.

"You're such a jerk, Kevin," Suzanne said.

"What did I do?" Kevin asked. "It's not like

I yanked the ring off Ms. Sweet's finger."

"But if you hadn't been trying to feed the fish, Ms. Sweet wouldn't have had to pull you away," Jeremy reminded him.

Katie frowned. She'd encouraged Kevin to drop some bread in the tank. So it was kind of her fault, too. Katie felt awful about that.

"This is just terrible," Becky exclaimed. "An engagement ring is just about the most important piece of jewelry there is. I, personally, can't wait to get one." She smiled at Jeremy.

Jeremy turned beet red and walked away.

"It's not Kevin's fault. He didn't mean for this to happen," Ms. Sweet said. Then she hurried off to find a guard.

"You guys have been so jealous about our engagement party," Suzanne said. "Maybe Kevin was trying to ruin things."

"Suzanne, that's ridiculous," Katie said.

"Yeah," Kevin added. "Who cares about your dumb old party, anyway?"

"It is not dumb!" Suzanne shouted back.

"Okay, kids, this isn't helping," Mr. G. said, stepping between Kevin and Suzanne. Then he turned to Ms. Sweet, who was back with a guard beside her.

Ms. Sweet was saying to the guard, "I'm quite sure my engagement ring slipped off and fell into the tank. Could you ask one of the divers to look for it for me?"

The guard looked at her. "Do you know where the ring is?" he asked her.

Ms. Sweet shook her head. "No. Not

exactly. But I was standing right here when it happened."

"Where did it land?" he asked.

Ms. Sweet shrugged. "I don't know. But I'm sure it can be spotted. The diamond is brand-new and very shiny."

"The divers are pretty busy right now, lady," the guard said. "They have a lot of fish to care for. If you knew where the ring was, that would be one thing. But they can't just take the time to look for it now. Maybe after we close they could take a quick look around for you."

Once again, Ms. Sweet looked as though she was going to cry. Katie felt really bad for her. But there was nothing Katie—or anyone else—could do for her right now.

"Oh. Okay. Well, would you ask them to do that?" Ms. Sweet asked him.

The guard nodded. "Sure thing, lady. Just write your name and phone number on this pad. If they find the ring in there, they'll call you."

Katie looked at the big tank. It was filled with plants and fish, and gravel and shells on the bottom. It would be really hard to find a diamond in all of that.

From the look on Ms. Sweet's face, Katie could tell she was thinking the exact same thing.

"Oh man, this is so bad," Katie heard Suzanne say to Becky.

"Ms. Sweet must feel just awful," Becky replied.

"We can't have a party for her tomorrow," Miriam added. "She'll be too sad to celebrate."

"But we have to have the party," Suzanne told her. "I'm supposed to be baking the cake with my mom this afternoon. Oh, how could Kevin do this to me!"

"To *you*?" Katie asked.

Suzanne blushed. "I mean to Ms. Sweet. This party is all about her, of course."

"Oh, *of course*," Katie replied.

"Why are you acting like you care, anyway?" Suzanne asked Katie. "Your class isn't even going to be there."

"You're right," Katie replied angrily. She turned and stomped off. Suzanne was being really nasty. She didn't want to be around her anymore.

Besides, seeing all the water around her was making Katie thirsty. She looked around for a sign for a water fountain. There was one nearby, just around the corner.

Katie knew she probably should ask Mr. G. for permission, but he was all caught up in helping Ms. Sweet. Anyway, she'd be back in a second.

Katie walked around the corner. She was happy to see that no one else was waiting for the water fountain. In fact, there was no one else around. Katie bent down and took a long sip of water from the fountain.

Just then, she felt a cool breeze blowing on the back of her neck.

That was weird. There weren't any open

windows or fans blowing.

The breeze got stronger, blowing hard and cold against Katie's back—and nowhere else.

Katie gulped. This was no ordinary wind. This was the magic wind!

"Oh no! Not now!" Katie cried out. "Not during a field trip!"

But there was no stopping the magic wind. It grew more and more powerful. The tornado whipped around wildly, blowing Katie's bright red hair all around her face.

The magic wind was so strong that Katie was sure it was going to blow her away.

But then it stopped. Just like that.

The magic wind was gone. And so was Katie Kazoo.

She'd turned into someone else . . . switch-eroo!

But who?

Chapter 7

The first thing Katie noticed was that she didn't have to open her eyes to see who she was. Her eyes were already wide open. Of course, that was because she didn't seem to have any eyelids.

Katie tried to look down to see what clothes she was wearing. Maybe that would give her a clue to who she'd switcherooed into.

But Katie couldn't bend her neck. She didn't even have a neck. So there was no way to look down at her fins.

Wait a minute. Her *fins*? People didn't have fins.

But fish do. And that was what Katie had

become—a fish. And not just any fish. Right now, Katie was hiding in the tentacles of a sea anemone. That could mean only one thing. Katie had turned into a clown fish. The very same clown fish she had frightened before.

Now it was Katie's turn to be frightened. *Really* frightened!

Katie wasn't an especially good swimmer. She'd only made it to the intermediate group at camp. She wasn't especially good at holding her breath, either. And that was something you had to do if you were under water.

Well, actually, if you were a fish you didn't have to hold your breath at all. Katie had learned that fish could breathe under water. And they were naturally good swimmers. Which meant Katie the clown fish was going to be fine.

Just then, another orange-and-white clown fish swam in front of Katie. It was happily darting back and forth between the sea plants that lined the aquarium. In and out it swam,

zigzagging happily through the water.

That sure looked like fun!

Katie moved her tail and fins quickly and swam up beside the other clown fish. Now there were two beautiful orange-and-white fish zipping through the water.

Before long, several clown fish joined in their game. They zoomed through the plants, one after another, as if they were playing a game of wild underwater tag!

As the water bubbled, Katie let out a little fish giggle. The fish in her school weren't all that different from the kids in her real school. They loved to play. The only good thing about a fish school was they could play all day. At Katie's school . . .

School! Katie stopped swimming. She'd just remembered that all her friends were outside the tank. Katie had wandered off without asking Mr. G. for permission. Now he was probably worrying about her—or even mad at her.

But it hadn't been her fault. It was the magic wind's fault that she wasn't with her class outside the tank.

Of course, she couldn't explain that to Mr. G. He wouldn't believe her anyway. Katie wouldn't have believed it, either—if it didn't keep happening to her.

I wonder if they can see me in here, Katie thought. Swishing her fins, she swam toward what seemed to be the glass wall of the aquarium. Her fish eyes allowed her to look in all directions except right behind her. But she couldn't see very clearly. In fact, she could only see a few feet ahead of herself.

The closer she got to the wall, the more she could see. She couldn't make out any faces, but she was pretty sure that there were people on the other side of the glass. Maybe they were her friends.

"Hey, look at me!" Katie tried to shout out as she flicked her tail up and flipped over in the water. "I'm just clown-fishing around!"

But of course, no actual sounds came out of Katie's fish face—just a bunch of bubbles.

"I can stand on my head!" Katie tried to say, moving so her head was facing the ground. "And I can do a triple twist!" she continued, turning her fish body round and round like a whirlpool.

Wow! This sure was fun.

Then suddenly, a dark shadow fell over Katie. She looked up just in time to see a huge nurse shark. And even with her fish eyes, she could clearly see those giant teeth—fish-eating teeth—heading right for her!

Katie gulped. This was soooooo not good!

Chapter 8

Any second now, Katie was going to become the shark's main course. It was swimming faster now, its big mouth wide open. Man, those teeth looked sharp.

Katie wanted to scream for help. But she was a fish. She couldn't scream.

The shark came closer.

Katie swished her fins as fast as she could. But the big fish was much faster than she was.

The shark came closer, still.

Just then, Katie's fish eyes spotted a big white sea anemone just a few inches away. *A safe base, just like in the game.*

Quickly, Katie burrowed herself deep into

the anemone's white tentacles. The shark swam right by without even stopping.

"It works!" Katie shouted out with excitement. Of course, no sounds actually came out of her mouth. But a whole lot of water bubbles blew all around her.

Katie's little fish heart was pounding. That had been so scary. Suddenly, she didn't want to do any more twists or somersaults in the water. She didn't want to play tag with the other clown fish.

She just wanted to be Katie Kazoo again— a ten-year-old girl who was on the *other side* of the tank.

But for now, she was a clown fish. And she couldn't hide in the sea anemone forever. Katie didn't know if sea anemones could get mad, but just in case, she didn't want to overstay her welcome.

Katie poked her head out to make sure the shark was gone. Once she was certain it was safe, she swam back out into the open water.

Then she looked around for the other members of the clown fish school. She didn't see any of them. She was all alone in this part of the tank.

Just then, something else caught her eye. Something bright and shiny. Right there, on the bottom, near a pretty starfish. What was it?

Katie the clown fish swam over to investigate. Now the shiny object became clear to her. A shiny rock, attached to a gold circle.

It took a moment before her little fish brain understood what she was looking at. The object was a ring. *And not just any ring!*

It was Ms. Sweet's engagement ring.

Katie began whirling and twirling excitedly in the water. She'd found Ms. Sweet's ring. She knew exactly where it was. This was so great.

Or was it?

Sure, Katie knew where the ring was. But she couldn't tell anyone. As long as Katie was a fish, Ms. Sweet's diamond engagement ring would be buried treasure at the bottom of the sea—er, aquarium.

Before she could think what to do, Katie felt a sudden change in the water around her. It was moving.

Oh no! Was another shark coming?

The water grew cooler, almost cold, as it blew around her tail fins. Katie didn't like the feeling at all. It was creepy—like icy fingers pounding on her little fish spine.

Katie looked around. None of the plants around her seemed to be moving with the blowing water.

None of the other sea creatures seemed to feel the breeze either. The starfish was still sitting quietly on the ground. And the sea anemone's tentacles were perfectly still.

It seemed like the wind was only blowing on Katie the clown fish. Which made sense because this was no ordinary wind. This was the magic wind.

The magic wind was just as powerful underwater as it was outside in the air. A moment later, the wind was blowing so wildly that Katie thought her tiny fish body would be blown right out of the tank.

She wished she could shut her eyes in fear—but she couldn't. She had to face this tornado with both eyes wide open. Round and round it blew, circling wildly about Katie.

And then it stopped. Just like that.

The magic wind was gone.

Chapter 9

And Katie Kazoo was back!

"Katie, what's all over your shirt?" Suzanne asked as Katie looked around a moment later.

Katie breathed a sigh of relief as she stared into Suzanne's face. She had never been so happy to see her best friend in her whole life! "Oh, that's just water," she told Suzanne. "I think it must be from the water fountain over there."

"Where else could it be from?" Suzanne said sarcastically. "It's not like you took a swim in the tank or anything."

Katie grinned slightly to herself. Then she

looked down at the school of clown fish. One of them was swimming around in circles, as if it was trying to figure out what had just happened in the tank.

Poor little fish. There was no way Katie could explain this to them.

Or to anybody else, for that matter. "No," she told Suzanne. "Of course I didn't go in there."

"This trip has turned out to be just awful, hasn't it?" Becky remarked.

"Ms. Sweet's party is ruined," Suzanne said.

Ms. Sweet! Katie had almost forgotten.

"Hey, I think I know where Ms. Sweet's ring is!" Katie shouted out excitedly.

Everyone stopped talking and stared at her.

"Katie, this is no time for jokes," Mr. G. warned.

"I'm not joking," Katie assured him. "Look. See? It's right down there, by the starfish."

"Which starfish?" Suzanne asked. She sounded like she didn't believe Katie at all. "There are, like, a million of them down there."

Katie pointed down toward the bottom of the tank. "The starfish near the white sea anemone where I was . . . I mean, where *that orange clown fish* was hiding." Whoops. That had been a close one.

"Show me, please," Ms. Sweet asked Katie, grabbing her by the hand and pulling her down the ramp toward the bottom of the tank.

The other kids and Mr. G. all hurried close behind them. In a flash, the whole fourth grade was on the ground floor of the aquarium, staring at the starfish through the glass.

"See, over there," Katie said, pointing right at the ring.

"Oh my goodness, you're right!" Ms. Sweet exclaimed. "I can see it sparkling on top of the gravel. I have to go tell that guard. He said the divers would get the ring if I knew exactly where it was. And now I do."

"I'll go tell him," Kevin assured Ms. Sweet. Katie could tell by the look on his face that he was very relieved. Now he wouldn't be hated by all of class 4B anymore.

"I'll go with him," Mr. G. added. He smiled at Ms. Sweet. "You and Katie just stay right here and keep an eye on that ring."

A few moments later, a diver in a black wet suit appeared in the tank. The kids all watched as she swam along with the fish and sharks, traveling toward where the ring was.

"It's right there!" Suzanne said. She banged on the glass. "Don't worry, Ms. Sweet, *I'll* make sure she doesn't miss it."

"Suzanne, stop banging on that glass," Katie insisted. "You might scare a fish so badly, it'll swim right into a shark's mouth."

"Oh, you don't have to worry about that," the guard told Katie. "The divers feed the sharks plenty of food. None of the predators hunt for prey because they're not hungry. All of our fish are safe in there."

Wow. Katie felt much better. She hadn't put that clown fish in any danger after all.

"But that doesn't mean you can bang on the glass, young lady," the guard continued, turning toward Suzanne. "It upsets the fish. That's why it's against the rules."

A moment later, the diver swam up to the glass so that she was face to face with Ms. Sweet. She held the ring up so she could see it.

Ms. Sweet smiled brightly. She mouthed the words "thank you" to the diver. The diver gave her a thumbs-up and then swam toward the top of the tank. A moment later, Ms. Sweet had her ring back.

The grateful teacher turned and gave Katie a big hug. "Katie, you're amazing!" she exclaimed. "How did you ever spot my little ring in that big tank? I would think you'd practically have to be right next to it to see it."

Katie smiled slightly. Ms. Sweet had no idea how true that was. "I guess I was just lucky," she said.

"No. *I* was lucky," Ms. Sweet replied.

"So is class 4B!" Suzanne exclaimed. "Now we can have my . . . I mean *your* engagement party, Ms. Sweet."

"I think we should invite class 4A to the party, too," Ms. Sweet said. "After all, Katie's in class 4A. And she's the one who saved the day."

"I guess," Suzanne said with a sigh. "But I don't know if there will be enough cake for all of them. My recipe only makes enough for our class."

"Don't worry about that," Ms. Sweet told Suzanne. "I'll take care of the food."

"Oh, this is going to be fun!" Katie exclaimed. She grinned at Suzanne, Miriam, and Becky. "Now we can all party together."

Miriam and Becky smiled back at her right away. It took Suzanne a little while to force a grin.

Chapter 10

"This is so much fun!" Katie squealed, taking another bite of her blue raspberry ice cream. "Oh yum! There was a green gummy fish in that spoonful." She smiled. "Even a vegetarian like me can eat these fish!"

Suzanne grinned. "You see, we have fun in our class, too," she told Katie. "We may not sit in beanbag chairs or play fish tag, but we have awesome parties."

Now Katie understood why Suzanne had wanted this party to be just for her class. Maybe the kids in class 4A did brag a little too much about the way-cool learning adventures Mr. G. was always thinking up.

"You sure do," Katie agreed with Suzanne. "I really love that Ms. Sweet gave her engagement party a fish theme."

"So do I," Jeremy agreed. "I never knew fish could be so delicious," he added, sliding a cherry-red gummy fish into his mouth.

"I think I'd like an aquarium theme for my engagement party one day," Becky cooed, glancing at Jeremy.

Jeremy rolled his eyes. "I'm gonna go get some goldfish crackers," he said as he hurried away.

"Hey, you guys, do you know what sea horses wear on their feet?" Kadeem shouted out.

"What?" Andy Epstein asked him.

"Horseshoe crabs!" Kadeem answered with a laugh.

Everyone else laughed, too.

Katie waited for George to come back with a joke of his own. But he didn't say anything. So Kadeem told another one. "What do you get when you cross a turtle with an electric eel?" he asked.

"What?" Emma S. asked him.

"Shell shock!" Kadeem told her.

Everyone laughed even harder.

But still, not a sound was heard from George.

"What's with George?" Katie whispered to Kevin.

"I don't know," Kevin said. "It's not like him to pass on a joke-off with Kadeem."

Just then Ms. Sweet walked over to where Katie was standing. "I just wanted to thank you again, Katie," the teacher told her. Ms. Sweet held out her hand. The ring sparkled on her finger. "I don't know what I would have done if I'd lost this ring forever."

Suzanne wrapped her arm around Katie's

shoulders. "My best friend saved the day," she boasted. "Of course, *I* taught her everything she knows."

"What's that supposed to mean?" Becky asked.

"I was the one who taught her to play I Spy," Suzanne explained. "We used to play it in the car. Of course, I always won."

"But Katie won when it really counted," Emma W. said, pointing to Ms. Sweet's ring.

Suzanne frowned. She opened her mouth to say something, but she was drowned out by the sound of Miriam screaming.

"Oooooo! That's so gross, George!" she shouted. "Get it away from me."

"What's the matter, Miriam?" he asked her. "Don't you like the under-the-sea environment I made? Come on. Take a bite!"

"Yuck! Get that away from me!" Miriam squealed as she ran as far from George as she could.

Katie looked into the bowl George was

carrying. He'd filled it with blue raspberry ice cream, gummy fish, goldfish crackers, and blue punch. It was all mushed together. Now Katie understood why George hadn't bothered with the joke-off.

"Let me see *you* eat it," Miriam called from the other side of the room. "I bet you won't put one spoonful of that mess into your mouth."

But Miriam was wrong. George scooped up a big spoonful of the ice-cream-cracker-candy-

punch slop, and shoved it into his mouth.

"Ooo. Nasty," Miriam said. She looked like she was going to be sick.

Katie laughed. It was a lot more fun pretending to be under the sea than to really be there. She blinked her eyes a few times, just enjoying the fact that she had eyelids again.

Yep, it was definitely more fun being Katie Kazoo than a clown fish. In fact, if it were up to her, Katie wouldn't switch places with anyone.

But it wasn't really up to her at all. And at just that moment, Katie felt a cold wind blowing on the back of her neck. She jumped up, startled.

Could the magic wind be back so soon?

Would it come here now, in front of all these people?

"Katie, will you shut the window, please?" Ms. Sweet called from across the room. "It's a little windy in here."

Phew. Katie gave a big sigh of relief. It

wasn't the magic wind at all. It was just a regular old wind. Which meant Katie would stay herself.

At least for now.

Go Fish!

Katie and her pals sure learned a lot about fish during their trip to the aquarium. Now it's your turn to take the bait and check out this list of fin . . . uh . . . er . . . *fun* fish facts!

1. Scientists believe that there are more than twenty-eight *thousand* different fish species!
2. One fish can actually walk on dry land! It's called the climbing perch. This fish will walk on land in search of water when its water hole dries up.
3. The heaviest fish ever caught was an

ocean sunfish. That whopper of a fish weighed 4,928 pounds!

4. When it comes to fish, the sailfish beats them all! It can swim up to sixty-eight miles per hour—faster than a car on the highway.

5. The slowest fish is the sea horse, which moves less than one-tenth of a mile per hour.

6. Fish don't actually sleep. But they do rest. When they are resting, some fish just float calmly, others wedge themselves into a spot in the mud or coral, and others actually build themselves little nests.

7. The largest fish is the whale shark, which can grow as big as fifty feet long.

8. The eye of a giant squid can reach fifteen inches in diameter. That's as big as a basketball!

9. One ocean sunfish can lay up to five

million eggs at one time!

10. Goldfish have toothlike structures in the back of their throats! They use them to grind their food. When old teeth fall out, new ones grow in.

About the Author

NANCY KRULIK is the author of more than 150 books for children and young adults, including three *New York Times* bestsellers. She lives in New York City with her husband, composer Daniel Burwasser, their children, Amanda and Ian, and Pepper, a chocolate and white spaniel mix. When she's not busy writing the *Katie Kazoo, Switcheroo* series, Nancy loves swimming, reading, and going to the movies.

✕   ✕   ✕

About the Illustrators

JOHN & WENDY'S art has been featured in other books for children, in magazines, on stationery, and on toys. When they are not drawing Katie and her friends, they like to paint, take photographs, travel, and play music in their rock 'n' roll band. They live and work in Brooklyn, New York.